Jennifer
the Hairstylist
Fairy

To Lizzie with love

Special thanks to Rachel Elliot

ISBN 978-0-545-48488-6

12 11 10 9 8 7 6 5 4 3 2 1   13 14 15 16 17 18/0

Printed in the U.S.A.   40

This edition first printing, July 2013

Jennifer
the Hairstylist
Fairy

by Daisy Meadows

SCHOLASTIC INC.

The Fairyland Palace

Tippington Fountains
SHOPPING CENTER

Top Hats & Tiaras

FASHION

HARTLEY'S

↑ Ice Blue
Hair Salon

Fashion Show

TIPPINGTON TOYS

Ice Blue
booth ←

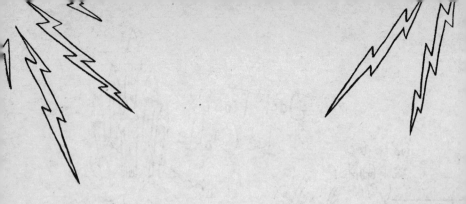

I'm the king of designer fashion,
Looking stylish is my passion.
Ice Blue's the name of my fashion line,
The designs are fabulous and they're all mine!

Some people think my clothes are odd,
But I will get the fashion world's nod.
Fashion Fairy magic will make my dream come true —
Soon everyone will wear Ice Blue!

Contents

Surprise in the Salon

Kirsty Tate and her best friend, Rachel Walker, gazed into the salon mirrors with excitement. They were sitting side by side, waiting to have their hair cut in the coolest salon in town — Snip & Clip.

"What's it going to be, girls?" asked Blair, the head hairstylist.

"I just want a trim," said Kirsty.

"What about you, Rachel?" asked Claire, the other stylist. "Are you going to try something more daring?"

Rachel's eyes sparkled as she looked at Claire in the mirror.

"I'd really love to have lots of tiny braids all over my head," she said. "Could you do that?"

"There's nothing that Claire can't do with hair!" said Blair with a laugh. "Let's get started."

The girls looked down at the cart that stood between them. It was full of special hairdressing scissors, combs and brushes,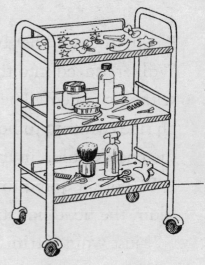

pretty barrettes, headbands, and jewels. They looked up and smiled at each other.

"I love getting my hair done," said Rachel. "It's even more fun when you're here with me!"

Kirsty was spending the fall break in Tippington with Rachel. As a special treat, Mrs. Walker had brought them to the new salon in the Tippington Fountains Shopping Center. Mrs. Walker was reading a magazine in the waiting area. She was planning to have her hair styled for a party that she and Mr. Walker were going to that night.

"Tippington Fountains is the best mall ever," said Kirsty. "We're so lucky — we've visited every single day since it opened!"

The gleaming new chrome and glass shopping mall had had its grand opening at the start of the week.

"Are you girls involved in the design competition?" asked Blair.

He snipped at Kirsty's hair and then paused, frowning at his scissors.

"They certainly are," said Mrs.  Walker, looking at them proudly. "They were both chosen to model their outfits in the fashion show at the end of the week!"

"Wow!" said Claire as she tugged at the tangles in Rachel's curly blond hair.

"You must have done a great job. Isn't the competition being judged by Ella McCauley, the famous designer?"

"Yes, and also Jessica Jarvis, the supermodel," said Rachel, nodding. "They were really nice at the design workshop."

"So, tell us about your outfits," said Blair.

"I made a dress out of colorful scarves, with a long, flowy skirt," said Kirsty. "Rachel painted a glittery rainbow on her old jeans. They look so cool now!"

"I love doing that," said Claire with a

smile. "It's so much fun bringing an old outfit back to life."

"We could show you how to do some great hairstyles for the fashion show," said Blair.

"Absolutely," Claire agreed. She did a few test braids in Rachel's hair. "I have to find a way to get these tangles out of your hair, Rachel. I'm just going to the storeroom to get some detangling spray."

"I'll come, too," said Blair. "I need a new pair of scissors. Every pair I pick up seems to be dull!"

Claire and Blair walked into the storeroom just as Mrs. Walker gasped in the waiting area. She jumped up and came over to the girls.

"Look at this!" she said, showing them the magazine she had been reading.

It was the latest issue of *The Fountains Fashion News*. The day before, Rachel and Kirsty had helped the magazine's reporter, Nicki Anderson, interview Ella McCauley.

"Ooh, is the article in there already?" asked Rachel.

Mrs. Walker nodded.

"It's really interesting," she said. "Good job, both of you! It's a real shame they couldn't find a better photo of Ella, though."

"What do you mean?" asked Kirsty.

Mrs. Walker handed the magazine to

Kirsty. Kirsty and Rachel gasped. Ella's hair looked awful!

"It looks like she just got out of bed," said Rachel. "Ella usually looks so elegant. She didn't look that messy yesterday."

Kirsty looked closely at the photo.

"That's funny," she said. "It's almost as if her hair has a blue shadow to it!"

She turned the page and let out a cry of surprise. There was a photo of their supermodel friend, Jessica Jarvis, whose hair was pulled back in a sloppy ponytail.

"Her hair is definitely blue," said Mrs. Walker. "I don't think it looks very nice, do you?"

Rachel and Kirsty exchanged a worried glance. Could this be the work of Jack Frost and his goblins?

A Tangled Problem

"Blue hair must be the latest fad," said Mrs. Walker. "But I don't think it's a good idea for the party we're going to tonight!" Laughing, she walked back to the waiting area.

"I bet this blue hair has something to do with Jack Frost," said Rachel thoughtfully, tapping the picture of Jessica Jarvis with her finger.

Earlier in the week, Kirsty and Rachel had visited Fairyland to see their fairy friends in a fashion show. Everyone was having a wonderful time until Jack Frost and his goblins barged in. They were modeling crazy, mismatched blue outfits that Jack Frost had designed. He had created his own designer label called Ice Blue.

"Do you remember what Jack Frost said?" asked Kirsty. "He wants everyone in the human world and Fairyland to wear blue so they'll all look like him."

Rachel nodded, looking serious. Jack Frost had stolen the Fashion Fairies' magical objects with a bolt of icy magic. Then he had taken them to Tippington

Fountains Shopping Center. But the fairies needed their objects in order to take care of fashion in both the human world and in Fairyland.

"We've already helped the Fashion Fairies find four of their missing objects," said Kirsty. "We just have to keep looking — we can't let Jack Frost turn everything blue!"

"Let's search the mall as soon as our hair is finished," said Rachel, glancing down at the cart. "Hey, look! The barrettes are glowing!"

The tiny hair clips were glowing red, blue, green, and silver. Then they rose into the air in a little swirl of color, and Jennifer the

Hairstylist Fairy popped out from underneath them! The barrettes dropped back to the cart, and Jennifer brushed a little fairy dust from her pretty red top and purple shorts.

"Hi, Jennifer!" said Kirsty, who was very excited to see the little fairy.

"Hi, girls!" said Jennifer, flicking a lock of her red hair back over her shoulder. "I have some news about my magic hairbrush. Jack Frost and the goblins are using it to turn everyone's hair blue!"

"That must be why the photographs in the magazine looked so strange!" Rachel exclaimed.

The girls quickly explained what they had seen in the magazine, and Jennifer looked worried.

"He wants everyone's hair to match his Ice Blue designer clothes," she said. "I have to stop him — but I don't know how."

"We'll help you," Kirsty promised. "I know we can find the magic hairbrush if we work together."

Just then, the storeroom door opened.

"Claire and Blair are coming," said Rachel. "Quick, Jennifer — hide!"

Jennifer quickly darted into Kirsty's pocket as the stylists walked over.

"OK, let's create some fabulous hairstyles!" said Blair with a grin.

Claire sprayed some detangling spray in Rachel's hair and continued braiding it, while Blair snipped at Kirsty's locks.

Blair kept smiling, but it was obvious to the girls that something was very wrong. Rachel's curls kept springing out of the braids, and Blair couldn't seem to cut Kirsty's hair to the same length on both sides.

At last, most of Rachel's hair was braided and Kirsty's trim was almost the same length all the way around. Claire checked her watch.

"We have to start on our next appointments now, girls," she said. "I'm sorry — we don't have time to show you any styles for the fashion show, and I know we haven't done a very good job on your hair."

She looked upset, and Rachel squeezed her hand. She knew it wasn't Claire's fault. Jack Frost and his goblins were causing all the trouble!

"It's all right," she said. "Please don't be upset about it. Maybe things will get better later."

"Yes, as soon as we find Jennifer's magic hairbrush," said Kirsty in a whisper. "Where could it be?"

"Mrs. Walker, would you like to come over?" said Blair, pulling out another chair as the girls stood up.

Mrs. Walker sat down eagerly, but when she saw the girls' hair her smile faded.

"Oh," she said, sounding surprised. "That wasn't quite what I had in mind."

"Please don't worry, Mom," said Rachel, kissing her mother's cheek. "I'm sure your hairstyle will look amazing."

"Can we look around the mall while you're getting your hair cut?" Kirsty asked. "We could meet you back here later."

Mrs. Walker agreed, and the girls hurried out of the salon as Blair started to work on her hair.

"Mom wants her hair to look really elegant for the party tonight," said Rachel as soon as they were out of earshot. "Kirsty, we *have* to get Jennifer's magic hairbrush back — and soon!"

Everyone's Got the Blues!

Rachel and Kirsty walked slowly past the long row of stores at Tippington Fountains. The mall was very busy. Suddenly, Kirsty grabbed Rachel's arm.

"Look over there," she said. "That woman in the café has blue hair."

"You're right," said Rachel. "And so does the waitress who's serving her — look!"

Three giggling girls walked past with their blue hair pulled back in pigtails. A man in skinny jeans and with a crazy blue crew cut hurried out of a flower shop.

"They all seem to like their hair," said Kirsty. "Oh, look at that sweet dog!"

A little poodle was standing outside the Posh Puppies grooming salon, wagging her tail. Her fluffy fur was bright blue.

"Yes, but did you see her owners?" asked Rachel.

The man and the woman standing next to the poodle also had blue hair. It was piled up on top of their heads in fluffy balls.

"They look just like their dog," said Jennifer, peeking out of Kirsty's pocket. "Oh, things are getting worse. We have to find Jack Frost — and fast!"

The girls turned left and found themselves among the clothing and accessories stores. They looked at the window of Finishing Touch, the accessories store, and gasped. It was packed with blue-haired people who were eagerly buying blue barrettes, headbands, and ribbons to match their new hairstyles.

"I don't understand why they all look so happy," said Rachel. "Do you think they *wanted* blue hair?"

"I think it's the effect of my magic hairbrush," said Jennifer. "If it touches your hair, you will feel happy and beautiful no matter what."

Kirsty and Rachel reached the fountain in the middle of the mall. They paused to look at the splashing waterfall and all the bright tropical flowers. Then Kirsty glanced around and felt a little shiver go down her back.

"Rachel, did you notice?" she asked in a low voice. "*Everyone* has blue hair!"

Rachel turned on the spot, looking at the crowd rushing around them. Men, women, children, and dogs were hurrying this way and that, and almost all of them had blue hair.

"How is Jack Frost doing this?" she wondered aloud.

Then she noticed a man standing outside the Sweet Scoop Ice Cream Parlor. From the back, he looked very familiar.

"That's odd," she said with a little laugh. "From behind, that man looks almost exactly like my dad — except for his spiky blue hair!"

Then the man turned around, and Rachel and Kirsty gasped. It *was* Mr.

Walker — with a brand-new Jack Frost
hairstyle! He waved at them and smiled.

"Hello, girls!" he called, walking
toward them. "I was hoping I'd bump
into you. What do you think of my
new look?"

Neither of the girls could reply at first.
Kirsty was trying very hard not to laugh.
She pressed her lips together and blushed

from the
effort of
holding
in her
giggles.
Rachel
was
speechless
with shock.
What would

her mom say about her dad going to the party looking like that?

"The stylist said that the spikes make me look really cool," Mr. Walker went on. "It's . . . *different*," said Rachel, finding her voice at last. Kirsty gave a spluttering laugh and had to turn her face away. Luckily, Mr. Walker didn't notice. He was too busy looking up at the mall's TV screens. One of them was showing a flashy advertisement in blue and white.

DON'T BE SQUARE.
GO TO ICE BLUE HAIR!

"That's where I went," said Mr. Walker, pointing at the TV screen. "The stylist was amazingly quick. The place seemed very popular."

Kirsty stopped giggling at once, and the girls exchanged a secret glance. Ice Blue Hair must be the goblins' salon!

"Dad, we'd really like to go and see the new hair salon," said Rachel.

"I'm not surprised," said Mr. Walker, looking at Rachel's frizzy braids and Kirsty's uneven haircut. "I'm sure they'll solve all your hair problems. It's just down there on the left." He pointed down one of the walkways.

"Thanks, Dad," said Rachel. "See you later!"

The girls hurried down the walkway and saw a blue booth with a sign saying ICE BLUE HAIR SALON outside. A long, long line snaked all the way around the corner.

Two short people with clipboards were standing at the front of the line. They had long blue hair that swished across their faces, and they were busy writing down appointments. Kirsty and Rachel edged closer to hear what they were saying.

"Hey, you!" one of them screeched at
the girls. "Wait your turn! Get to the
back of the line!"

Kirsty's mouth fell open. Beneath the
swish of blue hair, she glimpsed a long
nose and a green face.

"It's a goblin!" she told Rachel. "In
fact, I think they're *both* goblins!"

Kirsty in Disguise

"Jennifer's magic hairbrush might be inside the booth," said Rachel. "Kirsty, we have to get past this line."

"I have an idea," whispered Jennifer from Kirsty's pocket. "Can you find somewhere to hide that's out of sight?"

The girls looked around, and then Rachel spotted a nearby pillar. The store

on the other side wasn't open yet, so if
they hid behind the pillar, no one would
be able to see them.

"Over here," she said, pulling Kirsty by
the hand.

As soon as it was safe, Jennifer fluttered
out of Kirsty's pocket and hovered in front
of the girls.

"If I turn you into fairies, we can try to
get inside the booth without being seen,"
she said.

Rachel and Kirsty
nodded eagerly.
It was always
exciting to turn
into fairies!
Jennifer waved
her wand, and a
puff of golden fairy

dust cascaded over the girls. As it sprinkled
down, they felt themselves growing
smaller. Sheer, delicate wings appeared
on their backs, and they flapped them
with delight.

"Follow me," said Jennifer.

The three friends darted up
to the ceiling of the mall,
and then flew above
the booth. It had
no roof, and
they could see a
goblin hairstylist
working on a
customer inside.

"Let's get
closer," said Kirsty.

They fluttered
down until they were

just above the booth. The goblin inside was spraying the customer's hair blue, but he kept gazing at himself in the mirror and stroking his own flowing

blue locks. "That goblin's hair looks pretty goofy," Rachel whispered. "Can you see the magic hairbrush?" asked Kirsty. Jennifer shook her head. "I'm sure it's here, though," she said. One of the goblins with a clipboard suddenly poked his head into the booth.

"Hurry up!" he yelled.
"There's a huge line out here,
you know."

"I'm going as fast as I can,"
wailed the goblin hairdresser.

The other goblin
disappeared, but a few
seconds later he was back.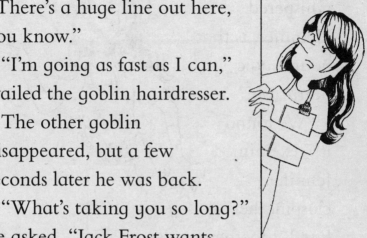

"What's taking you so long?"
he asked. "Jack Frost wants
everyone in the mall to have blue hair by
the end of the day."

"I only have two hands!" snapped the
stylist, sounding stressed.

He raised his hands to shoo the other
goblin out — and Rachel spotted a
glowing hairbrush sticking out of his
apron pocket!

"Look!" she whispered. "Jennifer, is that your magic hairbrush?"

"We found it!" exclaimed Jennifer, clasping her hands together. "But how are we going to get it away from the goblin?"

"I have an idea," said Kirsty. "Let's fly down into the booth and hide. If Jennifer can disguise me as a goblin, maybe he'll let me take over the styling."

The three little fairies dropped down into the booth and hid behind the full-

length mirror in the corner. They saw
the goblin take out a pair of scissors and
start to trim the customer's hair. Quickly,
Jennifer waved her wand over Kirsty's
head and said a spell:

"While the stylist gives a trim
Change fairy fair to goblin grim.
Give her skin of greenish hue
And don't forget her hair of blue!"

At once, Kirsty's fairy wings
disappeared and she grew to goblin-size.

Her skin turned green and her nose became long and pointy. Finally, her hair turned ice-blue. Kirsty gave a little twirl. The transformation was complete!

"How do I look?" she asked with a grin.

"Awful," said Rachel, smiling at her. "It's perfect!"

Kirsty waited until the customer got up to leave. Then, before the next customer could come in, she stepped out from her hiding place. Rachel and Jennifer watched from behind the mirror, keeping their fingers crossed for their friend.

"I've come to give you a break," said Kirsty to the goblin. "If you want, I'll take the next customer. Just give me the scissors and the hairbrush."

She reached out her hand, and Rachel and Jennifer held their breath. The goblin seemed to be thinking about it. His hand moved toward the hairbrush in his pocket . . . but then he shook his head.

"Jack Frost said that I'm the only one allowed to do hair," he

said, pulling the brush through his own blue locks.

"You look tired. Maybe I could be your assistant?" Kirsty suggested. The goblin walked over to the full-length mirror and gazed at himself. "No," he said. "I'm the only goblin with the skills to be a stylist."

Kirsty bit her lip. Rachel and Jennifer were just on the other side of that mirror, and Jennifer's golden fairy glow was lighting up the bottom edge. Kirsty hoped that the goblin would be too busy admiring himself to notice, but when he looked down at his humongous feet, he gave a yelp of surprise.

"What's that?" he demanded, pointing at the golden glow. "What's going on?"

Wig
Worries

Rachel and Jennifer swooped out from
behind the mirror.

"Quick, grab the magic hairbrush!"
Jennifer cried.

"Fairies!" squealed the goblin,
clutching the glittering hairbrush in his
hands. "Leave me alone!"

He ran out of the booth and vanished,

disappearing into the crowd of shoppers. "I'll follow him!" Rachel exclaimed.

She darted after the goblin as Jennifer waved her wand and turned Kirsty back into a fairy. Then they followed Rachel as fast as they could. She was flying high above the crowd, close to the ceiling of the mall where no one would see her.

"Can you see him?" Kirsty asked her best friend as soon as they reached her.

"Yes, he just ran into Posh Puppies," said Rachel. "Come on!"

The three friends swooped down and entered the dog-grooming salon. It was

very noisy inside, with the sound of
hairdryers and the happy yaps of
pampered pets. Suddenly, there was an
uproar of barks from the far end of the
salon, and the girls saw a swish of long
blue hair. All the dogs in the salon
started to bark and race toward the far
corner.

"Stop!" squealed the
owner, as a poodle
bounded over
her head.

"Calm
down!" cried
an assistant,
as a shampoo-
covered Pekingese
sprang out of
her arms.

"This is all the goblin's fault!" Jennifer groaned.

There was now a squirming, hairy pile of sweet-smelling dogs in the corner. Not one of them was listening to the owner. Then the girls saw the blue-haired goblin scramble out from under the pile and run toward the door.

"Don't lose sight of him!" cried Kirsty.

They hurried out of the shop and
flitted above the shoppers again as the
goblin weaved his way through the
crowd far below.

"He went into Finishing Touch," said
Rachel.

The three friends flew down and
slipped inside the accessories store. They
were just in time to see
the goblin zip away,
still loosely holding
the magic hairbrush
in his hand. Rachel
swooped toward
him, hoping to
grab it. She
reached out, but
only managed to
grasp the end of

his long blue hair. To her astonishment, the hair started to slip off his head. It was a wig!

Rachel flew back up to Kirsty and Jennifer, who were hovering near the ceiling.

"It's no use," she said. "I couldn't get the hairbrush. But I found out that he's wearing a wig."

"Yes, and look how much he loves it," said Jennifer.

The goblin hadn't realized that the fairies were in the store with him. He was standing in front of a mirror,

straightening the
wig and patting
down some stray
strands of hair.

"That gives me
an idea," said
Kirsty. "We can't
get the hairbrush,
so let's try to get his wig, instead. Then
maybe he'll be willing to do a swap."

"Great plan!" said Rachel, smiling at
her friend. "Look, he's leaving — let's
follow him."

The goblin scurried out of the store
and disappeared into the Sweet Scoop
Ice Cream Parlor. Rachel, Kirsty, and
Jennifer hovered above the entrance.

"OK, Rachel, get ready," said Kirsty.
"As soon as he comes out, we'll swoop

down and pull off
his wig."

"And
remember, you
can't let anyone
see you," said
Jennifer.

The girls
nodded, not taking
their eyes off the entrance. Soon, the
goblin stepped out, looking all around to
try and spot the fairies.

"Now!" cried Kirsty.

She and Rachel zipped down and flew
underneath the ends of the wig so that
no one nearby would see them. Then
they pulled with all their fairy strength!

"YOWCH!" squawked the goblin as
his blue hair slipped off his head.

He grabbed at it and held on tightly.
Rachel and Kirsty tugged as hard as
they could, but the
goblin's grip
was too
strong.
With a
jerk, he
managed to
pull it out of
their hands. But
then he lost his
balance and fell
over! The wig flew
through the air and
landed in a trash can with a loud *SPLAT*.

The goblin wailed and scrambled to
his feet. He grabbed the wig out of the
can and put it back on his head. It was

smeared with scraps of food and sticky
ice-cream wrappers. The goblin sniffed
sadly and tucked the magic hairbrush
safely back into his pocket. Then he
shuffled over to the
waterfall, where
he began to try
to wash out
the mess.

Rachel
and Kirsty
felt terrible.
They flew
over to a
little ledge on
the inside of the
fountain, hidden
from the passing

shoppers. Jennifer came to join them, and they all looked up at the goblin.

"We're really sorry," said Kirsty. "We didn't mean to mess up your wig."

"It's ruined," said the goblin, sniffing again. "Pesky fairies."

Suddenly, Rachel had a wonderful idea.

"Listen," she said in a kind voice. "I think there's a way that we can all be happy again. Jennifer's magic can make your wig as good as new. All you have to do to is give her back her magic hairbrush. What do you say?"

Breaking the Spell

The goblin didn't need to think about it for even a second! He loved his wig more than anything he had ever owned. He immediately held out the magic hairbrush.

As soon as Jennifer touched the hairbrush, it shrank to fairy-size. Instantly, the goblin's long blue hair was clean and silky again. He squealed with delight and leaned over to see his reflection in the fountain pool.

Kirsty and Rachel turned to each other and smiled.

"Kirsty, your hair isn't crooked anymore," said Rachel. "It looks great!"

"And your braids are neat and straight," Kirsty added.

"That's the power of the magical hairbrush," said Jennifer, giving a little twirl of joy on the spot.

The goblin was trying out different hairstyles with his long blue hair. As he tied it in

pigtails, Jennifer took Kirsty and Rachel by the hands. "It's almost time for me to go back to Fairyland," she said. "I can't wait to tell the other Fashion Fairies the good news! But first, I need to turn you back into humans again."

She rose into the air and the girls followed her. From high above the mall, they could see that the shoppers no longer had blue hair.

"Thank goodness things are back to normal," said Kirsty.

"Look — the line is gone at the Ice Blue Hair Salon," Rachel noticed.

The goblins with clipboards were still standing outside the booth, shouting.

"Step right up, step right up, get your blue hair here!"

"Blue hair special today!"

But the passersby were just laughing and shaking their heads. Rachel, Kirsty, and Jennifer flew down behind the booth, where no one could see them. Then, with a wave of Jennifer's wand, the girls became human again.

"Thank you for helping me find my magic hairbrush," Jennifer said. "I'd

like to give you a special gift in
return — something you can wear at
the fashion show."

Two ribbons of fairy dust streamed
from her wand. One landed on Rachel's
head, and the other
on Kirsty's head.
Instantly, two
pretty violet
barrettes
appeared
in their
hair. They
sparkled with
fairy dust.

"Thank you,"
said Rachel, her eyes shining with
delight.

"They're beautiful," Kirsty added.

"Good-bye, girls," said Jennifer, with a beaming smile. "Good luck at the fashion show!"

"Good-bye, Jennifer!" said the girls. "Thank you!"

The little fairy disappeared with a tiny sparkling pop, and Rachel and Kirsty stepped out from behind the booth. The goblins with clipboards were trudging away, muttering grouchily at each other.

"Come on," said Rachel, looking at her watch. "It's time to meet Mom at the salon."

The girls hurried back through the mall until they reached Snip & Clip. Mrs. Walker was just walking out of the salon. Her hair was pulled back in an elegant, sleek style.

"Mom, you look gorgeous!" Rachel exclaimed, giving her a kiss.

"Your hair looks fabulous," Kirsty agreed.

"Yours, too," said Mrs. Walker happily. "I'm not sure why I thought it looked bad earlier."

"Hello!" called a cheerful voice.

They turned and saw Mr. Walker coming toward them.

"Dad, what happened to your cool spiky blue hair?" Rachel asked with a grin.

His hair was back to normal. Mrs. Walker looked confused.

"I can't imagine your dad ever having spiky blue hair," she said.

"You don't have to imagine it," said Kirsty, stifling a giggle. "Look up there!"

She pointed at the mall TV screen. There was a huge close-up of Mr. Walker from earlier that day — complete with his spiky blue hairdo!

As Mrs. Walker giggled helplessly, Mr. Walker's cheeks turned pink.

"I don't know what came over me," he said. "It was as if I was under a spell that made me want to have blue hair."

"Thank goodness the spell wore off!" said Mrs. Walker, kissing him on the cheek.

Rachel and Kirsty exchanged a secret glance. Mr. Walker had no idea that his joke about the spell was true!

"We still have to find two more magic objects to break Jack Frost's Ice Blue spell completely," said Kirsty in a whisper.

"We can do it," said Rachel, her voice confident. "After our adventures today, I feel like we can do anything!"

RAINBOW magic™

THE FASHION FAIRIES

Kirsty and Rachel helped Jennifer
find her magic brush.
Now it's time for them to help

Brooke
the Photographer Fairy!

Read on for a special sneak peek. . . .

Photo Fiasco

"This place is so beautiful," said Kirsty Tate, gazing around at the lush green grass, the bright flowers, and the potted palms. "Isn't it funny seeing a garden up so high!"

She was standing in the middle of the roof garden on top of the brand-new Tippington Fountains Shopping Center.

The glass-fronted Roof Garden Café was at the far end. Next to the café was a glass elevator that took visitors down to the mall.

"It must be even prettier when the sun's shining," replied her best friend, Rachel Walker. "All the glass must really sparkle."

They both looked up at the gray rain clouds that were gathering overhead.

"Yes, it's too bad that it isn't a sunny day," Kirsty agreed.

All week long, the girls had been involved in the design competition at the new shopping mall. There was a fashion show planned for the next day to celebrate the end of the mall's first week.

"I think this is the best place to have a photo shoot, even if the weather isn't perfect," said Rachel with a smile.

Kirsty's and Rachel's outfits had been among those chosen to be in the fashion show. Today, the winners were taking part in a photo shoot for *The Fountains Fashion News* magazine. Supermodel Jessica Jarvis and designer Ella McCauley were there, too. They had been special guests at the shopping mall all week, and now they were helping the kids make sure that their colorful, imaginative clothes looked as good as possible. Kirsty was wearing the dress that she had made out of scarves, and Rachel had put on her rainbow-painted jeans.

Cam Carson, the photographer, was busy organizing the winners into groups.

RAINBOW magic™

There's Magic in Every Series!

The Rainbow Fairies
The Weather Fairies
The Jewel Fairies
The Pet Fairies
The Fun Day Fairies
The Petal Fairies
The Dance Fairies
The Music Fairies
The Sports Fairies
The Party Fairies
The Ocean Fairies
The Night Fairies
The Magical Animal Fairies
The Princess Fairies
The Superstar Fairies

Read them all!

HiT entertainment

scholastic.com
rainbowmagiconline.com

RMFAIRY7

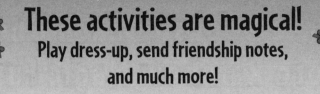

These activities are magical!
Play dress-up, send friendship notes, and much more!

RAINBOW magic™

SPECIAL EDITION

Three Books in Each One— More Rainbow Magic Fun!

Joy the Summer Vacation Fairy
Holly the Christmas Fairy
Kylie the Carnival Fairy
Stella the Star Fairy
Shannon the Ocean Fairy
Trixie the Halloween Fairy
Gabriella the Snow Kingdom Fairy
Juliet the Valentine Fairy
Mia the Bridesmaid Fairy
Flora the Dress-Up Fairy
Paige the Christmas Play Fairy
Emma the Easter Fairy
Cara the Camp Fairy
Destiny the Rock Star Fairy
Belle the Birthday Fairy
Olympia the Games Fairy
Selena the Sleepover Fairy
Cheryl the Christmas Tree Fairy
Florence the Friendship Fairy
Lindsay the Luck Fairy

■SCHOLASTIC

scholastic.com
rainbowmagiconline.com

HIT entertainment

RMSPECIAL10